INTRODUCTION

Magnetism is a force that acts between magnets. You may think of magnets as toys that pick up nails or other bits of iron and steel, but magnetism is an important force in nature. Magnetism is all around us and we use it every day. Magnets come in all shapes and sizes. Magnets are used in telephones, television sets and radios; they can work giant machines, they can seek out north and they can push and pull other magnets. In fact, the world has become a different place since magnetism was first discovered. People once believed that magnets had mystical powers and could heal the sick. It was when sailors first learned how to magnetize a compass needle, however, that the age of science began. The Magnetic North Pole of the Earth was located in 1831 by Sir James Clark Ross, and almost 100 years later, in 1909, the Magnetic South Pole was located by a party led by Lord Shackleton. Nowadays, we know much more about the Earth and magnetism. We even rely on magnetism to produce large amounts of electricity for us. As you find out more about magnetism and magnets, you will discover that they are not only very useful, but a great deal of fun too!

Introduction

Bright ideas for further projects

Science projects with practical experiments

Why it works explaining the science ideas

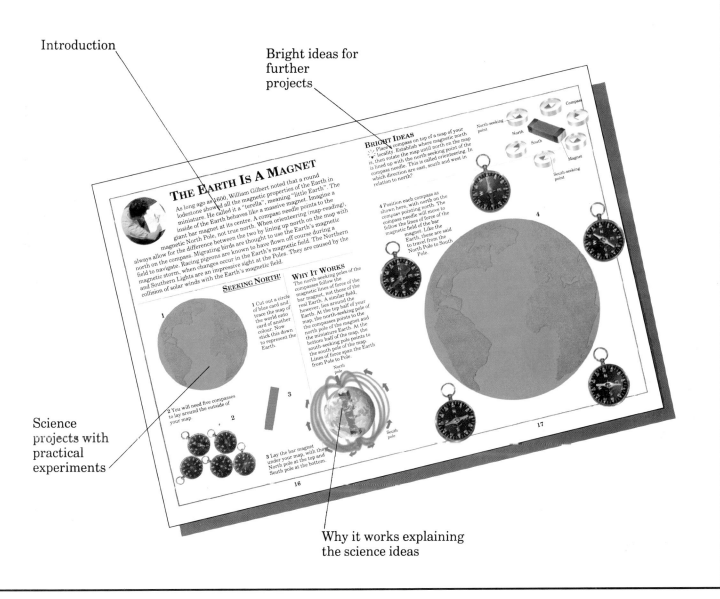

THE WORKSHOP

A science workshop is a place to test ideas, perform experiments and make discoveries. To prove many scientific facts you don't need a lot of fancy equipment. In fact, everything you need for a basic workshop can be found around your home or school. Read through these pages and then use your imagination to add to your "home laboratory". Make sure that you are aware of relevant safety rules and look after the environment. A science experiment is an activity that involves the use of certain basic rules to test a hypothesis. A qualitative approach involves observation. A quantitative approach involves measurement. Remember, one of the keys to being a creative scientist is to keep experimenting. This means experimenting with equipment as well as with ideas to give you the most accurate results. In this way you will build up your workshop as you go along.

MAKING THE MODELS

Before you begin, read through all the steps. Then make a list of the things you need and collect them together. Next, think about the project so that you have a clear idea of what you are about to do. Finally, take your time in putting the pieces together. You will find that your projects work best if you wait while glue or paint dries. If something goes wrong, retrace your steps. And, if you can't fix it, start over again. Every scientist makes mistakes, but the best ones know when to begin again!

GENERAL TIPS

There are at least two parts to every experiment: experimenting with materials and testing a science "fact". If you don't have all the materials, experiment with others instead. For example if you can't find any sand, use sawdust or shredded paper instead. Once you've finished experimenting, read your notes thoroughly and think about what happened, evaluating your measurements and observations. What conclusions can you draw from your results?

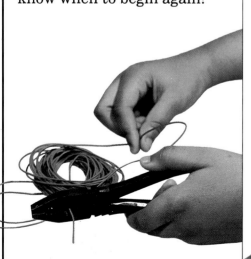

SAFETY WARNINGS

Make sure that an adult knows what you are doing at all times. Filing an iron nail to make iron filings can be dangerous. Ask an adult to do this for you. In the experiments that use electricity, always use a battery of 1.5 volts. Never use mains electricity! Always be careful with scissors. If you spill any water, wipe it up right away. Slippery surfaces are dangerous. Clean up your workshop when you finish!

EXPERIMENTING

Always conduct a "fair test". This means changing one thing at a time for each stage of an experiment. In this way you can always tell which change caused a different result. As you go along, record what you see and compare your results with what you thought would happen before you began. Ask questions such as "why?", "how?" and "what if?". Then test your model and write down the answers you arrive at. Compare your results to those of your friends or classmates.

MAGNETIC ATTRACTION

Archaeologists and beachcombers often make use of metal detectors to locate buried objects or treasure. Materials are either magnetic or non-magnetic. Most, but not all, metals are magnetic. Iron has the strongest magnetic attraction. Nickel and cobalt are also magnetic, as are the alloys, or mixtures, of these metals. Aluminium, copper and gold are non-magnetic. Magnetic ferrites (metals containing iron) can be used to make hard magnets, like the fridge stickers pictured here. These are known as permanent magnets. Soft magnets are temporary and are easy to magnetize and de-magnetize. Magnetic materials can be easily separated from other materials. When aluminium cans are recycled, they are sorted from other metals by using a magnet. You can make your own metal detector with an ordinary magnet. See if you can find any buried treasure!

SECRETS IN THE SAND

2 Hold the card in place by attaching small strips of paper to the cone and winding them tightly around the stick. Now decorate the card with paint or coloured paper.

1 Make a circle, 10 cm across out of coloured card and cut a slit from the edge to the centre. Overlap the two ends and glue, to create a flat cone. Push one end of a stick through the centre and attach a button magnet to the stick with plasticine.

3 Half fill a shallow container with clean sand. Bury a variety of objects in the sand, metals and non-metals.

4 Move your metal detector slowly above the surface of the sand. Try it at various heights. You will soon discover how low you must hold it to attract objects.

WHY IT WORKS

A magnet exerts a force on a nearby piece of magnetic material by turning it into a weak magnet – this is magnetic induction. A magnet is made up of many tiny parts called domains. Each one is like a mini-magnet, and they all point in the same direction. The domains in a metal are jumbled up. When a magnet comes into contact with the metal, the domains line up and the metal becomes magnetized. A strong magnet can act over quite a distance. Each object picked up from the sand is a temporary magnet because the domains inside become aligned.

Magnetized metal

Unmagnetized metal

BRIGHT IDEAS

Predict which objects you expect your magnet to pick up - you may be surprised! How near to the sand must the magnet be held before it picks anything up? At what height does it fail to attract any of the hidden objects? Keep a record of your results.

Which objects does your magnet pick up? Which are left buried in the sand? What does this tell you about them? Do any of the magnetic objects keep their magnetism and attract other objects?

Try a different kind of magnet. Can you pick up any more objects with it? What happens if you add more sand to the container?

Find out which other metals are non-magnetic. Collect some empty drinks cans and sort them with a magnet. Remember aluminium is non-magnetic. Save them for recycling.

4

WHERE IS MAGNETISM?

Magnetite, or lodestone, is a naturally occurring magnetic ferrite. The first magnets were made by stroking magnetic materials with a lodestone. You will find magnets of many shapes and sizes – bar, horseshoe and button are only a few. Every magnet is surrounded by something called a magnetic field where magnetism is found.

The areas of the magnet where magnetism is at its strongest are called the poles. Every magnet has at least two poles. Poles are named after the direction they point in. These are north and south.

Iron filings

FLAT FIELDS

1 Place two bar magnets beneath a large sheet of paper, resting each end of the paper on a thin book. Position the magnets with unlike poles facing each other.

2

2 Ask a grown up to make some iron filings by filing down an iron nail. Now scatter them over the surface of the paper, around the positions of both magnets. Tap the paper gently and watch the magnetic fields form.

WHY IT WORKS

Magnetic lines of force run from north to south and they are strongest where the lines are closest together. This indicates where the poles of the magnet are located. Because like poles repel, for example two south poles, the magnetic fields of the magnets also repel each other. As the iron filings are magnetized they are drawn into the magnetic field, showing the lines of force around the magnet.

BRIGHT IDEAS

Move the two magnets so that like poles are facing each other. What do you notice about the shape of the magnetic field now?

Repeat the experiment with magnets of different shapes and observe the pattern of the magnetic field of each.

Hit a magnet with a hammer – what effect does this have on the magnet? Can you still show its magnetic field with the iron filings?

Lines of force

South

North

9

MAGNETIC FIELDS

The space around a permanent magnet in which its effects can be felt is called its magnetic field. A permanent magnet exerts a force that extends some distance from it in every direction. These invisible lines are like closed loops, with part of the loop inside the magnet and part forming the field outside. The lines of force never touch or cross. You have already seen how iron filings give a flat picture of a magnetic field. A magnetic field can cause a compass needle, which is itself a bar magnet, to move. The presence of a magnet near electrical equipment can create havoc, in the same way as the magnetic needle in a compass is made to move. Magnetic shields are designed to avoid such problems (see page 14). Using iron filings and oil you can demonstrate the three-dimensional nature of a magnetic field.

OIL FIELDS

1 Almost fill a see-through container with a clear, thick liquid like cooking oil or glycerine. Scatter iron filings into the liquid and gently stir the mixture with a stick to disperse the filings evenly.

2 Now place a bar magnet underneath the jar and allow the filings to settle. View them from above. You will see the magnetic field of the magnet as a three-dimensional pattern formed by the iron filings.

1

BRIGHT IDEAS

Try holding a horseshoe magnet against the outside of the jar. What effect does this have on the iron filings in the oil? Where are the lines of force closest together?

Jar

Oil

Iron filings

WHY IT WORKS

The iron filings become temporary magnets whilst inside the magnetic field of the bar magnet, bunching together where the field is strongest. The oil supports the filings in the shape they form around the magnet. The lines of force in a magnetic field move from north to south. Every magnet has a north and south pole at each end, like the Earth. As you can see from the shape appearing in the oil, magnetic lines of force are closest at the poles – this is where the magnet is strongest. The weakest part of a magnet is at its centre.

2

ATTRACTION AND REPULSION

Within its magnetic field a magnet will either attract or repel another magnet. If two metal objects attract each other it is difficult to tell which one is the magnet. The only true test of a magnet is to see if it is repelled by another magnet. A bar magnet has two poles, one "north" and one "south". If a bar magnet is broken in the middle, new poles will appear at the broken ends. As we know that like poles repel and unlike poles attract, it is wrong to describe the north-seeking point of a compass needle as "north". In fact, it is the south pole of the magnetic needle that is attracted to the Earth's magnetic north pole. Always use the term "north-seeking" to avoid confusion. Using the laws of magnetic attraction and repulsion, see if you can move a toy car around the track. The attraction and repulsion between the two magnets should be strong enough to push and pull the car. Maybe you can win a race?

TRACK EVENT

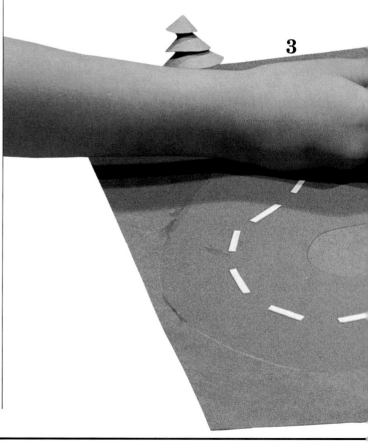

1

1 Firmly attach a bar magnet to the roof of a toy car. Use some strong sticky tape. Make sure that the magnet is well-balanced.

2 Cut out a race track from grey card and attach it with glue to a sheet of green card – make sure there are no bumps. Add some trees.

2

3 Place the car on the track. Hold one end of a bar magnet close to the end of the magnet at the rear of the car. If the car moves backwards turn the magnet you are holding round the other way. You can push or pull the car round the track by holding the magnet in different places.

3

WHY IT WORKS

Magnets can push or pull because like poles repel but unlike poles attract. This attraction and repulsion is strong enough to push and pull the car round the track.

When two north poles face each other the opposing magnetic fields cancel each other out – this is called the neutral point. The repulsion between two like poles is so strong, it is impossible to push them together. This magnetic force can be used to push the toy car round the track. In the same way, the attraction between opposite poles can be used to drag the car along.

BRIGHT IDEAS

☀ Suspend a small magnet above a needle attached by thread to a flat surface - watch the needle rise up into the air.

☀ Suspend a bar magnet freely. Close to it suspend a second magnet. Watch them move as the like poles pull away from each other.

MAGNETISM TRAVELS

A magnetic force can travel through many substances. It can even travel through water. Treasure on the sea-bed can be detected by a diver carrying an instrument called a magnetometer. The same is true of other non-magnetic materials – you have already seen how magnetic lines of force can travel through paper to the iron filings. What other materials do you think magnetism could travel through? Because tiny magnets as fine as powder are used to store images and sounds on tapes and computer disks, a magnetic field can interfere with the quality. The effect can only be lessened by placing another magnetic object within the magnetic field. This is a shield which cancels out the effect. Make this hockey game and prove that magnetism can travel through non-magnetic materials.

1 Cut out two figures holding hockey sticks from card. Colour them so that they are wearing different shirts. Behind each hockey stick attach a small magnet with plasticine.

BULLY-OFF!

2 Attach a bar magnet firmly to one end of two long sticks. These sticks can then be held underneath the "pitch" and used to move the players.

3 The hockey pitch can be made from a painted cardboard lid raised up on four wooden legs. Fold two strips of card to be the goalposts. Mark the centre line and circles with coloured tape. Put the "players" in position, facing each other. You can score goals using a ping-pong ball.

WHY IT WORKS

Non-magnetic materials allow a magnetic field to pass through them. A magnetic material will pick up the magnetic force and weaken it. Cardboard is not magnetic. It allows a magnetic force to pass through it. Distance is important. If the magnet is too far away or if the non-magnetic material is too thick, the effect of the magnet will not be felt. Some magnets are stronger than others. The weaker the magnet, the closer it must be held to the magnetic material. A strong magnet can be held further away because its magnetic field is larger.

BRIGHT IDEAS

Fill a plastic see-through container with water and attach a paperclip to the bottom with plasticine, as shown. Now take a cork and insert another paperclip to make a hook. Using a bar magnet on the outside of the container, see if you can drag the cork to the bottom and anchor it to the clip. See what other materials magnetism will work through. Try plastic, wood and china.

South pole

Magnet

Cardboard

Magnet

North pole

Plastic container

Water

Cork

Magnet

Paperclip

Plasticine

THE EARTH IS A MAGNET

As long ago as 1600, William Gilbert noted that a round lodestone showed all the magnetic properties of the Earth in miniature. He called it a "terella", meaning "little Earth". The inside of the Earth behaves like a massive magnet. Imagine a giant bar magnet at its centre. A compass needle points to the magnetic North Pole, not true north. When orienteering (map-reading), always allow for the difference between the two by lining up north on the map with north on the compass. Migrating birds are thought to use the Earth's magnetic field to navigate. Racing pigeons are known to have flown off course during a magnetic storm, when changes occur in the Earth's magnetic field. The Northern and Southern Lights are an impressive sight at the Poles. They are caused by the collision of solar winds with the Earth's magnetic field.

SEEKING NORTH!

1

1 Cut out a circle of blue card and trace the map of the world onto card of another colour. Now stick this down to represent the Earth.

2 You will need five compasses to lay around the outside of your map.

2

3

3 Lay the bar magnet under your map, with the North pole at the top and South pole at the bottom.

WHY IT WORKS

The north-seeking poles of the compasses follow the magnetic lines of force of the bar magnet, not those of the real Earth. A similar field, however, lies around the Earth. At the top half of your map, the north-seeking pole of the compasses points to the north pole of the magnet and the miniature Earth. At the bottom half of the map, the south-seeking pole points to the south pole of the map. Lines of force span the Earth from Pole to Pole.

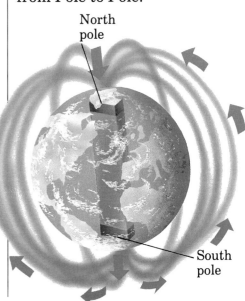

North pole

South pole

BRIGHT IDEAS

Place a compass on top of a map of your locality. Establish where magnetic north is, then rotate the map until north on the map is lined up with the north-seeking point of the compass needle. This is called orienteering. In which direction are east, south and west in relation to north?

North-seeking point

Compass

North

South

Magnet

South-seeking point

4 Position each compass as shown here, with north on the compass pointing north. The compass needle will move to follow the lines of force of the magnetic field of the bar magnet. Like the Earth, these are said to travel from North Pole to South Pole.

4

FOLLOWING MAGNETS

Almost 2000 years ago, the Chinese knew how to make a simple compass by suspending a long, thin piece of magnetite or lodestone. Later, sailors used a lodestone to magnetize the needle for a ship's compass. Compasses were being used in China in the eleventh century. The Italian explorer, Amerigo Vespucci, whose name was mistakenly given to America, understood the concept of a magnetic North Pole. It was not until the sixteenth century, however, that it was fully accepted. Christopher Columbus was unable to navigate with total accuracy, because his compass readings were inaccurate – probably due to magnetic interference. Today, many large ships have a gyrocompass. This gives a bearing (compass direction) in relation to true north. Make your own simple compass by magnetizing a needle.

CRAFT A COMPASS

1 You will need a waterproof plate, a cork, a magnet and a steel needle. Half fill the plate with clean water. Holding the magnet the same way all the time, stroke the needle with it at least 50 times. Always stroke in the same direction and lift the magnet off the needle each time you want to begin another stroke.

2 The needle has now been magnetized permanently, because it is steel. Push it through the cork, so that the cork balances on the water evenly. Allow the water to become absolutely still. The needle will seek out the Earth's Magnetic North Pole to point north. Make sure there are no magnetic materials nearby.

WHY IT WORKS

By stroking a permanent magnet along the needle, the domains inside become aligned. This turns the needle into a magnet, too. Any magnet free to turn horizontally will settle pointing north/south, as the north-seeking pole is attracted to the Earth's Magnetic North Pole.

Permanent magnet

Direction of stroke

Cross-section of magnetized needle

Unmagnetized needle

BRIGHT IDEAS

Find a way to mark your compass clearly with the four compass directions. You could even design a compass rose.

Make a different kind of compass by pivoting a magnetized needle on folded card on top of a stick. The stick is kept upright inside a container using plasticine.

Place a paper clip underneath a metal lid made from a magnetic metal. Try to move the paper clip from beneath the lid with a magnet. You will find it difficult. Why is this?

Using a bar magnet you can show how a compass needle seeks out north. Suspend the magnet freely - make sure there are no magnets nearby - the magnet will rotate until it points north-south. The north-seeking pole (which is the south pole of the magnet) will face north.

Try floating a bar magnet on wood or cork in a bowl of water. What do you expect to happen?

Draw an eight-point compass. What is the size of the angle between each compass point?

Plastic container

Needle

Card

Stick

Plasticine

ELECTROMAGNETS

The discovery of electromagnets in the 1800s was the first step in investigating the relationship between electricity and magnetism. In 1820, a Danish physicist, Hans Christian Oersted discovered that a wire conducting an electric current produces a surrounding magnetic field. We now know that when electricity flows through a coil of wire wrapped around a soft iron core it creates a strong magnet, called an electromagnet. Electromagnets are used in many appliances and machines. Door bells, telephones and burglar alarms are only a few. The most powerful electromagnets are those used in scrapyards to lift heavy pieces of metal. You can build your own pick-up using an electromagnet.

A MAGNETIC PICK-UP

1 Use two boxes to make the crane. Make the arm from card, using a cotton reel and pencil to create a lever. Wind insulated wire (blue) around an iron nail 50 times.

1

2 Take one end of the blue wire to the battery in the base and the other to a drawing pin in the side of the body. Attach a paperclip to this pin to create a switch (as shown), and insert another pin within reach of the clip.

2

3 To this second pin attach the red wire, taking the other end to the battery. When the paperclip joins both drawing pins, electricity flows through the wires causing the nail to become magnetized.

3

Flow of electricity

Magnetized nail

Domains

Wire

Unmagnetized nail

WHY IT WORKS

An electromagnet is a coil of wire around an iron core. When an electric current flows through the coil a strong magnetic field is created. The strength of the field depends upon the "push" of the current – the voltage. The strength of an electromagnet can be increased by the addition of extra turns of wire to the coil, by increasing the voltage in the circuit and by bringing the poles of the magnet closer together. If steel and not iron is used the metal will stay permanently magnetized. Iron becomes a temporary magnet. This means that when the current is switched off, the magnetic field disappears.

BRIGHT IDEAS

Wind about 60 turns of insulated wire around a steel nail. Connect the end to the battery and turn on the power. You have made a magnet. Make extra turns in the wire round the nail. Add another battery to the circuit. Observe any changes.

USING MAGNETISM

The magnets used by scientists vary in size, shape and strength. With the development of electricity, the electromagnet is now part of much modern equipment, both scientific and domestic. Numerous gadgets and machines work for us because of magnetism. They range from a lid-holding can opener to an atom-smashing machine, called a particle accelerator. In our homes, weak magnets help to hold refrigerator doors firmly shut. In factories, magnetic conveyor belts transport iron and steel cans. Precision instruments may have light-weight moving parts suspended inside them with a magnet. We all make use of machines like the ticket machines pictured here. They can sort coins into their different values. You can also sort coins using your own magnetic slot machine.

A MAGNETIC SLOT MACHINE

2 Now fit the card diagonally inside a tall box as shown. Hinge one side of the box to allow access.

2

1

1 Take a piece of stiff card and attach a strong magnet underneath with sticky tape. Attach it to the left side of the piece of card.

WHY IT WORKS

When you drop the coins and washers into the slot, they travel down the shute, passing over the magnet. The metal washers, which are magnetic, are diverted by the magnetic field and fall into the left-hand compartment. The coins, which are not magnetic, carry on straight down the shute landing in the right-hand compartment. A real vending machine tests the coins with an electric current. It can sort the coins by testing the amount of electricity conducted.

Slot

Coin

Direction of magnetic washers

Washer

BRIGHT IDEAS

 If you push the "coins" through the slot with greater force does it make any difference? Examine your results and draw conclusions from them.

With small button magnets you can make some magnetic stickers. Cut out letters or shapes and colour them in. Use them to make a board game.

Draw your own weather map on magnetic material and design some weather symbols that can be mounted on small magnets.

3 Cut an opening at the bottom of the box, the same width as the stiff card. Fit a cardboard tray divided into sections, as shown. Enclose the top of the box, cutting a slit adjacent to the top of the stiff, sloping card. Make the slit long enough to allow coins to be pushed through.

4 Finish off your machine by decorating the outside. Collect as many different coins and metal washers as you can and roll each through the machine.

3

FUN WITH MAGNETS

Now you know more about magnets, how many do you think you could spot around your home and school? Maybe you have fridge stickers or a magnetic notice board. Somebody you know may have a magnetic catch on their bag or maybe you own a magnetic travel game like chess or draughts. If you want them to be, magnets can be lots of fun. But you must look after them! All magnets become weaker over time and should be stored carefully, in pairs, with unlike poles together. Every magnet should have a piece of soft iron, called a keeper, across each end. Be careful not to drop your magnets, as this can result in them losing their magnetic powers. Magnetic sculptures can be bought in shops, but you can make your own with paperclips. Gather together your magnets and let's have some fun!

MAGNETIC SCULPTURE

Place a bar magnet beneath an upturned paper plate. Collect together some paperclips and scatter them on top of the plate. The magnetic field of the magnet travels through the plate, magnetizing the paper clips. Now you can build up a sculpture, making all sorts of different shapes. How high can you build? What happens when you take the magnet away?

BEARDED FACE

Draw and colour in a man's face on a paper plate. Leave out his hair, eyebrows and moustache. Now place some iron filings on the plate. Keeping the plate level, lift it in one hand and hold a magnet underneath with the other. By moving the magnet around under the plate, you can make hair grow. You could even create a hair-raising monster! To make another picture, just remove the magnet and shake.

BUZZING BEE

To suspend your buzzing bee, join two sticks together with sticky tape, as shown. Make a hole in an upturned flower pot holder and insert the longest stick.

Cut a ping pong ball in half and paint the bee's stripes. Add some wings, eyes and antennae.

Now take a bar magnet and cover it in brown paper. Stand it upright in the centre of your base, fixing it with plasticine. This will be your flower stem.

Suspend the bee from the pole with a piece of cotton, and attach a button magnet inside the body with plasticine.

Cut out some petals from coloured paper and make a large flower, as shown.

Suspend your bee from the pole so that it hangs just above the flower. Watch the bee buzz around the flower. Once in motion, it will continue to fly as it is repeatedly attracted and repelled by the bar magnet in the stem. Is there any pattern to the bee's buzzing? What if you turn the bar magnet the other way up? Does the pattern change?

31

Scientific Terms

ELECTRIC MOTOR A machine that uses a magnet to to turn electricity into movement.

ELECTROMAGNETISM The relationship between electricity and magnetism – one can be used to produce the other.

GYROCOMPASS A compass that points to true north because it does not use magnetism.

LODESTONE A piece of magnetite, a magnetic rock used as a compass by early explorers.

MAGNETIC FIELD The area surounding a magnet or an electric current that attracts or repels magnetic materials

MAGNETIC INDUCTION Making a temporary magnet out of a magnetic material by placing it within the magnetic field of a permanent magnet.

MAGNETIC NORTH POLE The point on the Earth's surface where magnetism is concentrated. The magnetic north pole is about 1600 kilometres from the geographic north pole.

MAGNETIC SHIELD A magnetic material placed within a magnetic field to cancel out the effect of another magnet.

MAGNETISM An invisible force that attracts or repels magnetic materials.

MAGNETIZE Making a magnet by stroking or touching a magnetic material with a permanent magnet.

MAGNETOMETER An instrument for measuring the direction or intensity of a magnetic field.

NEUTRAL POINT The point where two opposing magnetic fields cancel each other out as a result of the repulsion of like poles.

SOLENOID A cylindrical coil of wire which acts as a magnet when an electric currrent is passed through it.

Index

PRINTED IN BELGIUM BY
proost
INTERNATIONAL BOOK PRODUCTION